A Wonderful Place

Come dream of a wonderful place.
We'll fly to a faraway land
　where hearts are so young,
　　and living is fun.
Come see if it just isn't so.

　Let's walk down the candy cane lane
　　and watch all the reindeer at play.
The sights you will see will fill you with glee.
Come see if it just isn't so.

　　A wonderful, wonderful place
　　　is Santa's white toyland.
　　There's never a sad-looking face
　　　in Santa's white toyland.

You're welcome to come one and all.
The Christmas Express waits your call.
We know you'll agree, it's heaven to see
　this wonderful, wonderful place.

BOOFO™
THE DOG THAT GOES
WHERE SANTA GOES

By Joseph P. King
and E. Del Thomas

Illustrated by Dick Dugan

PELICAN PUBLISHING COMPANY
Gretna 1997

TRADEMARK

To all the children of the world . . . to the young and the young at heart

Library of Congress Cataloging-in-Publication Data

King, Joseph P., 1929-
    Boofo : the dog that goes where Santa goes / by Joseph P. King and
E. Del Thomas ; illustrated by Dick Dugan.
        p.   cm.
    Summary: Boofo, a small dog found and taken in by Santa, helps the
elves make toys and gets to ride in the sleigh on Christmas Eve.
    ISBN 1-56554-295-9 (hc : alk. paper)
    [1. Dogs—Fiction. 2. Christmas—Fiction. 3. Santa Claus-
-Fiction.]   I. Thomas, E. Del. II. Dugan, Richard, ill.
III. Title.
PZ7.K5847Bo 1997
[E]—dc21   97-9055
                                                          CIP
                                                          AC

Printed in Hong Kong

Published by Pelican Publishing Company, Inc.
1101 Monroe Street, Gretna, Louisiana 70053

BOOFO™
THE DOG THAT GOES
WHERE SANTA GOES

To all the children of the world, the North Pole is a wonderful place indeed, for it is where Santa Claus lives.

Not long ago, Santa was taking a walk in the snowy forest with three special elves who were his constant companions. They were brothers. Mr. Bim was the youngest and kind of shy, grumpy Mr. Bam was next, and Mr. Boom was the oldest. He liked to be the leader (like most older children!).

After they had walked for a while, Santa paused and stared down at the ground. "What have we here?" he exclaimed, puzzled. Two large and very sad eyes peered out from a small quivering mound of snow.

With great tenderness Santa lifted the shivering pile to his chest.

Slowly and carefully he brushed the snow away.
"By jingle," chuckled Santa. "I believe it's a dog."
"It *is* a dog!" shouted Mr. Boom.
"A scrawny mutt," sniffed Mr. Bam.
They returned to Santa's house at once.

Santa quickly made a soft bed for the dog near the fireplace.
"Santa, I feel someone should watch the fire tonight," suggested Mr. Boom. "We wouldn't want it to go out."

"That's a good idea," said Santa. Mr. Boom proudly puffed his chest out.

The loving care given the sick dog soon made him well— perhaps too well for Mr. Bam's liking. "He is never still . . . running and jumping everywhere," he complained. "He's a troublemaker!" It was easy to tell Mr. Bam didn't like the dog. He was jealous of all the attention the puppy got.

"Nonsense!" shouted Mr. Boom. "Santa and I agree that he's just very happy."

Mr. Bam would try to scare the dog so it would leave him alone. "Boo!" he would shriek. At first, the dog would jump with fright and run away. Then he started answering each loud "Boo!" with a few playful barks. This made Mr. Bam even angrier, but it made Mr. Bim laugh.

"If we are kind and gentle to animals," Santa admonished, "we will find a true and happy friend. Please, Mr. Bam, try to be a little nicer."

"Exactly," bellowed Mr. Boom. Mr. Bam just scowled at the floor.

Mr. Bim, being the youngest, was a little timid. He often had good ideas but he didn't like attention, so he would whisper his thoughts to Mr. Boom. He was whispering now.

"True, true," nodded Mr. Boom. "My brother suggests we name the dog. He thinks the name should be—"

"Boofo!" chirped Mr. Bim happily. With that the dog jumped on Mr. Bim, knocking him playfully to the floor and licking his face.

Still Mr. Bam was unhappy. He felt that Boofo did not belong there. One night when everyone was asleep, he crept downstairs. He went to the front door and opened it. He hoped Boofo would go find some other house to bother.

That morning Boofo woke up early. He felt the chill from the open door. He wondered why it was open and went outside to find some answers.

Mr. Bim was always the first to awaken in the morning. He would hurry downstairs to see his new friend. Usually Boofo would run right to him.

But this morning was strangely quiet, and Boofo's bed was empty.

Mr. Bim called Boofo's name. He rushed about opening doors and looking in toy chests, but Boofo wasn't there.

When Mr. Bim couldn't find Boofo inside, he looked outside. But Boofo was nowhere to be found. Mr. Bim finally went back inside. With nothing else to do, he cried for his missing friend.

Awakened by the noise, Santa and the others appeared.

"My, my, Mr. Bim, what seems to be the trouble?" asked
Santa.

"You should feel sorry for waking us," added Mr. Bam
sharply. "And why on earth do you have the door open?" He
quickly slammed the door shut.

Mr. Bim clutched Mr. Boom's arm and whispered into his
ear. Mr. Boom was deeply moved. "Mr. Bim fears Boofo has
disappeared," he announced.

All day, everyone searched everywhere. (Mr. Bam didn't look very hard.) Still they could not find Boofo. Late that evening Mr. Boom cried out, "Has anyone seen Mr. Bim?" No one had.

"If he has gone to find Boofo, he may be in trouble," Mr. Boom wailed. "There is a terrible snowstorm!"

"You see!" shouted Mr. Bam. "That dog *continues* to make trouble, even *after* I've gotten rid of him!"

"Oh!" yelled Mr. Boom. "*You* left the door open! Shame on you, brother, shame on you!"

"Shh," said Santa. "I think I hear Boofo's bark!"

At once they all rushed out into the storm. They found Boofo digging frantically into a snowbank. "Look!" said Santa. "I see Mr. Bim's sweater!"

"Oh, what have I done?" moaned Mr. Bam. "What have I done?"

For the next few days Mr. Bim was given special care. Soon he was all better. Mr. Bam called everyone together. Hanging his head, he said, "I am very sorry I behaved so badly. Boofo, I was wrong about you. You saved my brother's life. I'm grateful and I promise to treat you better."

Boofo was so happy that he leaped up and began to lick Mr. Bam's face.

"All right," laughed Santa. "We are a happy family again. This is good because we must begin our important work—making this year's Christmas toys!"

The Workshop Song

Doodle-lee doo, doodle-lee doo
    there's lots of work to do.
Doodle-lee dum, doodle-lee dum
    we've got to get it done.
For Christmas Eve will soon be here
    and Santa's list is long.
So doodle-lee doo, doodle-lee dum
    let's sing the workshop song.
Doodle-lee dee, doodle-lee dee
    the workers all are we.
Doodle-lee dop, doodle-lee dop
    the wood we'll have to chop.
We'll nail the nails and glue the glue,
    we'll paint so happily.
So doodle-lee dee, doodle-lee dop
    we're busy as can be.
Be-doodle be-daddle ska-diddle dee dum
    be dee dee dee dee doo.
Be-doodle be-daddle ska-diddle dee doe
    be day be doo bee dum.
For Christmas Eve will soon be here
    and Santa's list is long, so
Doodle-lee doo, doodle-lee dum
    let's sing the workshop song.

The next morning Boofo was awakened suddenly by a sharp crackling noise. He was drawn to the workshop door by a bad smell and more sounds.

Boofo knew in a flash that there was something very wrong in the workshop. He barked and barked and barked. Everyone came running.

It was a fire! Mr. Boom took charge and directed the elves to fill buckets with water. Everyone worked as quickly as they could.

When the fire was finally out, Santa looked around. His workshop was a mess. The elves stood stunned, tears running down their cheeks.

"How bad is it?" Santa asked the weary Mr. Boom.

"We've lost a lot of toys," Mr. Boom replied, for once quiet. "And we had more this year than ever before."

"It will be close to impossible to get the toys done in time," Santa sighed.

Boofo suddenly jumped up on a work bench. In his mouth he held a hammer and a paint brush. On his head he wore an empty glue pot.

"Why," exclaimod Mr. Boom, "Boofo is telling us not to waste any time!"

Everyone cheered their agreement and Boofo began to bark loudly.

Santa's workshop hummed merrily once again. The elves put in long hours, working faster than ever.

This time, instead of getting in the way, Boofo helped. He would hold a glue pot or a bucket of paint in his mouth, or bring lists from Santa to the elves.

"More nails, Boofo," said Mr. Bam. "A hammer!" shouted Mr. Boom.

"Hurry everyone," urged Mr. Bim. "Tomorrow will be Christmas Eve!"

DECEMBER
23

A few hours later a relieved Santa announced, "We're done!"

"Here, here!" shouted the gathering of elves. Santa smiled in appreciation.

"To each of you I owe a lot," Santa said. " And I am thankful that Boofo was here to help us." The elves threw their hats high in the air and celebrated.

Boofo jumped up on Santa's lap. "You are truly a joy," said Santa.

" . . . gooooo!"

Off into the enchanted Christmas Eve sky soared the reindeer, the sleigh, Santa Claus, and Boofo. As they disappeared,
all the elves started singing:

"'Cause Boofo goes where Santa goes
    and children know where Boofo goes.
On Christmas Eve when all is dark
    children hear Boofo bark . . ."

So this Christmas Eve, listen very carefully. You may hear a dog barking faintly in the distance. It won't be the dog down the street, or in the next block.

It will be Boofo, Santa's trusted friend, helping Santa deliver your toys.